The Bedtime Mother Goose

Pictures by Ron Himler

 Golden Press • New York

Western Publishing Company, Inc.
Racine, Wisconsin

To bed, to bed
Says Sleepy-head.
Tarry a while, says Slow.
Put on the pan,
Says greedy Nan,
We'll sup before we go.

Sippity sup, sippity sup,
Bread and milk from a china cup;
Bread and milk from a bright silver spoon,
Made of a piece of the bright silver moon!
Sippity sup, sippity sup,
Sippity, sippity sup!

Polly put the kettle on,
Polly put the kettle on,
Polly put the kettle on,
We'll all have tea.

Sukey take it off again,
Sukey take it off again,
Sukey take it off again,
They've all gone away.

Blow the fire and make the toast,
Put the muffins down to roast;
Blow the fire and make the toast,
We'll all have tea.

Twinkle, twinkle, little star,
How I wonder what you are!
Up above the world so high,
Like a diamond in the sky.

When the blazing sun is gone,
When it nothing shines upon,
Then you show your little light,
Twinkle, twinkle, all the night.

Diddle, diddle, dumpling, my son John,
Went to bed with his trousers on;
One shoe off, and one shoe on;
Diddle, diddle, dumpling, my son John.

Go to bed, Tom,
Go to bed, Tom,
Tired or not, Tom,
Go to bed, Tom.

Sleep, baby, sleep,
Thy father guards the sheep;
Thy mother shakes the dreamland tree
And from it fall sweet dreams for thee,
Sleep, baby, sleep.

Sleep, baby, sleep,
Our cottage vale is deep;
The little lamb is on the green,
With woolly fleece so soft and clean,
Sleep, baby, sleep.

Sleep, baby, sleep,
Down where the woodbines creep;
Be always like the lamb so mild,
A kind and sweet and gentle child,
Sleep, baby, sleep.

The Man in the Moon
Looked out of the moon,
And this is what he said,
'Tis time that, now I'm getting up,
All babies went to bed.

Wee Willie Winkie runs through the town,
Upstairs and downstairs in his nightgown,
Rapping at the window, crying through the lock,
Are the children all in bed, for now it's eight o'clock?

Boys and girls, come out to play,
The moon does shine as bright as day;
Leave your supper and leave your sleep,
And come with your playfellows into the street.
Come with a whistle,
Come with a call,
Come with a good will or not at all.

Rub-a-dub-dub,
Three men in a tub,
And how do you think they got there?
The butcher, the baker,
The candlestick-maker,
They all jumped out of a rotten potato,
'Twas enough to make a man stare.

I saw a ship a-sailing,
A-sailing on the sea,
And oh but it was laden,
With pretty things for thee.

There were comfits in the cabin,
And apples in the hold;
The sails were made of silk,
And the masts were all of gold.

The four and twenty sailors
That stood between the decks,
Were four and twenty white mice
With chains about their necks.

The captain was a duck
With a packet on his back,
And when the ship began to move
The captain said Quack! Quack!

Humpty Dumpty
Sat on a wall,
Humpty Dumpty
Had a great fall,
All the King's horses and all the King's men,
Couldn't put Humpty together again.

The Queen of Hearts
She made some tarts,
All on a summer's day;
The Knave of Hearts
He stole the tarts,
And took them clean away.
The King of Hearts
Called for the tarts,
And beat the Knave full sore;
The Knave of Hearts
Brought back the tarts,
And vowed he'd steal no more.

See-saw, sacradown.
Which is the way to London town?
One foot up and the other foot down,
That is the way to London town.

Pussycat, pussycat, where have you been?
I've been to London to visit the Queen.
Pussycat, pussycat, what did you there?
I frightened a little mouse under her chair.

There was a crooked man, and he walked a crooked mile;
He found a crooked sixpence against a crooked stile;
He bought a crooked cat, which caught a crooked mouse,
And they all lived together in a little crooked house.

Sing a song of sixpence,
A pocket full of rye;
Four and twenty blackbirds
Baked in a pie.
When the pie was opened,
The birds began to sing;
Wasn't that a dainty dish
To set before the King?

The King was in the countinghouse,
Counting out his money;
The Queen was in the parlor,
Eating bread and honey.
The maid was in the garden,
Hanging out the clothes,
When along came a blackbird,
And snipped off her nose.

Old King Cole was a merry old soul,
And a merry old soul was he.
He called for his pipe and he called for his bowl,
And he called for his fiddlers three.

Every fiddler, he had a fine fiddle,
And a very fine fiddle had he.
Twee, tweedle-dee, tweedle-dee, went the fiddlers.
Oh there's none so rare
As can compare
With King Cole and his fiddlers three!

A cat came fiddling out of a barn,
With a pair of bagpipes under her arm;
She could sing nothing but fiddle-de-dee,
The mouse has married the bumblebee;
Pipe, cat; dance, mouse;
We'll have a wedding at our good house.

Three young rats with black felt hats,
Three young ducks with white straw flats,
Three young dogs with curling tails,
Three young cats with semi-veils,
Went out to walk with two young pigs
In satin vests and sorrel wigs.
But suddenly it chanced to rain
And so they all went home again.

There was a maid on Scrabble Hill,
And if not dead, she lives there still.
She grew so tall she reached the sky,
And on the moon hung clothes to dry.

There was an old woman tossed in a blanket,
Seventeen times as high as the moon;
But where she was going no mortal could tell,
For under her arm she carried a broom.
Old woman, old woman, old woman, said I!
Whither, ah whither, ah whither so high?
To sweep the cobwebs from the sky,
And I'll be with you by and by.

Hey diddle, diddle,
The cat and the fiddle,
The cow jumped over the moon;
The little dog laughed
To see such sport,
And the dish ran away with the spoon.

What did I dream? I do not know;
The fragments fly like chaff.
Yet strange my mind was tickled so,
I cannot help but laugh.